The Adventures of Goliath

On Their Own

Terrance Dicks

Illustrated by

Valerie Littlewood

The Adventures of Goliath

On Their Own

Terrance Dicks

Illustrated by
Valerie Littlewood

First edition for the United States and
the Philippines published 1993 by
Barron's Educational Series, Inc.

First published 1992 by Piccadilly Press Ltd.,
London, England

All inquiries should be addressed to:
Barron's Educational Series, Inc.
250 Wireless Boulevard
Hauppauge, New York 11788

International Standard Book No. 0-8120-1675-0

Library of Congress Catalog Card No. 93-19927

Library of Congress Cataloging-in-Publication Data
Dicks, Terrance.
    On their own / Terrance Dicks ; illustrated by Valerie
Littlewood.
        p.   cm. — (The Adventures of Goliath)
    Summary: At home on their own, David and his dog Goliath
try to catch a gang of robbers who have eluded the police.
    ISBN 0-8120-1675-0
    [1. Dogs—Fiction.   2. Mystery and detective stories.]
I. Littlewood, Valerie, ill.   II. Title.   III. Series: Dicks,
Terrance.   Adventures of Goliath.
PZ7.D56270n   1993
[Fic]—dc20   93-19927
                                                              CIP
                                                              AC

PRINTED IN THE UNITED STATES OF AMERICA
345 9770 987654321

CONTENTS

Page

1. Noises in the Night   1

2. Alarms and Excursions   11

3. On the Trail   23

4. The Mysterious Intruders   34

5. Goliath's Big Moment   44

Chapter One

Noises in the Night

"Well, that's it for tonight," said the handsome young TV show host. "And don't forget, the police are waiting for your calls in the case of the latest bank robbery ...." He gave a big toothy smile. "Above all, don't be alarmed or upset by what you've seen on our program."

David switched off the TV and turned to Goliath. "He spends the whole program telling us about robberies and

murders, then tells us not to worry about it! Oh well … how about a cup of cocoa before the movie starts? And a few cookies, of course!" Goliath, David's huge hairy dog, barked enthusiastically at the sound of the magic word "cookies."
"All right, come on then," said David. He led the way out into the kitchen.

As they passed the bottom of the stairs, Goliath suddenly stopped, cocking his

head. "What's up boy?" asked David. Goliath whined uneasily. David listened. He heard footsteps, a thud, low muttering voices .... The thing was, there shouldn't have been any sounds. Although it was quite late at night, David and Goliath were in the house all alone ....

It all started when the peace of Sunday morning was broken by a phone call. David's mom had answered it, and David could hear her worried voice. When she put down the telephone, her face was white. "Gram's had an accident," she said.

"What?" said David's dad, throwing down his Sunday paper. "What kind of an accident?"

"Is she all right?" asked David.

Sensing the general excitement, Goliath barked noisily. "Keep quiet,

Goliath!" shouted David. "Tell us what happened, Mom."

David's mom drew a deep breath. "Luckily it's not too bad. She slipped in the kitchen and banged her elbow and head. Grandad called an ambulance and they took her to the hospital. Apparently they're keeping her in overnight. Grandad's pretty shaken up. I've got to get over there and look after him."

Everyone started talking at once and Goliath began barking again.

"All right, keep calm everyone," said David's dad. "Let's make a sensible plan."

The first part of the plan, rather to David's relief, was that since Sunday dinner was in the oven and nearly ready, they might as well eat it. The delicious smell of roast beef and roast potatoes was filling the house, and there was apple pie . . . . Right after dinner they'd set off to see Gram.

"I'd really like to stay the night," said David's mom.

"I could stay too and get to work from Grandad's," said his father. "But what about getting David back in time for school?" Gram and Grandad lived several hours' drive away.

David nobly offered to have a day off, but no one seemed to think this was a good idea.

"All right, then," he said. "The answer's obvious. You two go and Goliath and I will stay here. He's not exactly the sort of dog to take to a hospital for a visit anyway!"

Goliath dropped his head and tail and gave David a reproachful look.

"It would be a help not to have to take Goliath," admitted Dad. "But I don't like the idea of your staying in the house alone."

Mrs. Richards, their landlady, who lived in the upper part of the house, was away visiting a friend.

"I know," said David's mom. "I'll ask Susan to come and stay over. She can bring Billy and they can sleep in our spare room. She can get your supper and breakfast, and get you off to school." She jumped up and ran to the phone. Susan was a friend of Mom's who lived up the street. Billy was her lively three-year-old.

"I'm too big to need a babysitter," protested David. "I can manage perfectly well on my own."

"I'm sure you can," said Dad quietly. "But this way your mom won't be worrying about you as well as Gram."

David opened his mouth and then

shut it again. "All right," he said. "It'll be nice having young Billy over, won't it, Goliath? I guess you'll have to spend all evening giving him rides."

Goliath barked and wagged his tail, pleased that everyone seemed to be cheering up.

After a hurried dinner, David's mother and father drove away. David had volunteered to do all the dishes so they could leave quickly. When it was finished he awarded himself an extra slice of pie for good behavior and gave Goliath the beef bone. Soon after that they set off for the park for an afternoon of football with some of David's friends.

It was just starting to get dark when they got back. The phone was ringing, sounding strangely loud in the empty house. David rushed in and grabbed it.

"Hello?"

"Thank goodness! I've been trying to get you for ages . . . ." said a frantic voice. It was Susan from up the street.

"Sorry, I've been out. Aren't you supposed to be here by now?"

"It's little Billy, he's developed a fever and some kind of rash. I phoned the doctor and she said it's nothing serious, but he needs to be kept quiet. I honestly don't think he's up to coming over and spending the night in a strange bed, and besides if it *is* anything contagious . . . ."

"It's okay," interrupted David. "We'll be fine, you stay and look after Billy."

"Will you be all right on your own till your parents get back? Will they be very late?"

Suddenly David realized—Susan thought his parents were coming back that same night. He decided to let her keep thinking it—she had more than enough to worry about as it was. "Don't worry. We'll be fine," he repeated. "Tell Billy to get well soon and Goliath will give him some more rides."

Goliath, as usual, barked at the mention of his own name.

"I'm sure that'll make him feel better," said Susan, already sounding relieved. "Sorry about all this."

"No problem," said David. He said

goodbye and put down the phone. Then he turned to Goliath. "Well, it looks as if we're on our own after all!"

He went into the kitchen and put on the kettle. While it boiled he considered what to do next. Should he call his parents at Gram's? No, like Susan, they had enough to worry about. "I'll get myself some supper," he thought. "I'll spend a quiet evening at home with old Goliath."

David found he was really looking forward to spending the night in the house alone. It would be a bit of an adventure. But that, of course, was before he heard the sinister sounds . . . .

Chapter Two

Alarms and Excursions

The first part of the evening had gone strictly according to plan. David cooked himself a supper of bacon, eggs, and beans, raiding the freezer for ice cream for dessert. Goliath, of course, had his usual can of Wuffo.

There'd been a bit of excitement after supper. The burglar alarm had started ringing in the house across the street, which was one of the biggest and fanciest houses on the block. Some new people had just moved in there. David had occasionally seen the owner, a plump, dignified-looking little man, going to work wearing a hat and carrying an umbrella.

David knew some alarms were so sensitive that the least little thing set them off. He had often heard store alarms ringing and ringing away in the evenings, while everyone walked by, paying no attention. No one seemed to be paying any attention now. Suppose there really was a robbery?

David was just wondering whether he ought to call the police station when he heard a car pull up in the street outside. Peering out of the living room window, he saw a police car, light flashing away on top, parked outside the big house across the street. Two young policemen got out, one tall and thin, the other shorter and a bit chubby. They stood looking up at the house, which was all in darkness. They went up the walk and examined the front door. Then they disappeared around the back of the house for a minute. They reappeared, got back in their police car and drove away. Soon after that the alarm stopped ringing.

"The policemen found no sign of a break-in, and decided it was a false alarm," David told Goliath. "I guess they switched it off back at the station."

Goliath barked his agreement.

After supper, David settled down in front of the television. There was an old James Bond film, *Thunderball,* which he watched with great enjoyment, even though he'd seen it before. The next program was one of David's favorites, a true-crime documentary called *Crime*

Call. There was a murder, a drug-smuggling case, the exploits of a gang of crafty bank robbers, and a series of antiques robberies from suburban homes. At the end of the program David headed for the kitchen . . . . Then he heard those mysterious sounds . . . .

David stood at the foot of the stairs, listening hard. Beside him, Goliath listened too. The sounds came again—movement, a kind of scuffling sound, muttering, all mixed up together . . . . David realized the noises weren't coming from upstairs as he'd thought at first. They were coming from next door—and the house next door was empty! The "For Sale" sign had been up for weeks. Old Mr. MacGregor who used to live there had suddenly gotten fed up with the city and gone off to live with his son in the country, leaving the house, and all its contents, in the hands of a real estate agent. Mr. MacGregor had been a bit of a collector, and there was supposed to be some very valuable stuff in there. David's detective mind went to work again. "You know what happened, don't you, Goliath?"

Goliath cocked his head, looking puzzled.

"Well, the burglars tried to get in the house across the street. The alarm and then the police turning up scared them away. But they'd noticed the 'For Sale' sign next door, so they've decided to try their luck there." David gave Goliath a stern look. "Well, we know what to do now, don't we? We can't let our old friend Mr. MacGregor get robbed."

Goliath barked excitedly, aware that something was up.

"Exactly," said David. "We must call the police—just like they tell you on *Crime Call!*" He went to the telephone and dialed 911.

David and Goliath didn't have very long to wait. In a reassuringly short time the same police car pulled up in the street and the same two policemen climbed out. David and Goliath went out to meet them.

"This seems to be our night for your street," said the tall policeman.

"I know," said David. "I saw you earlier."

"You the one who called in?" said the chubby policeman.

"That's right."

"Been watching *Crime Call*, have you?"

"Yes, but . . ."

The policeman sighed. "Always the same on *Crime Call* night. Every nervous old lady in the country hears burglars under the bed and calls in."

"Well, I'm not a nervous old lady," said David indignantly. He hated it when grown-ups wouldn't take him seriously. "I tell you I heard noises from the house next door, movement and voices. Goliath heard it too, didn't you boy?"

Goliath woofed happily at the two policemen.

"We'll check it out," said the tall policeman. "Wait here."

Taking flashlights from their car, the two policemen went next door to Mr. MacGregor's house. As before, they checked the front door and windows, then went around to the back. David waited with Goliath outside his own house. It felt strange standing outside in the empty street. Beyond the streetlights the night was dark and stormy, and it was beginning to rain. Trees rustled, and David even thought he saw a figure lurking in the bushes.... The policemen were only gone for a few minutes and when they came back David asked eagerly, "Did you find anything?"

"Well, yes and no," said the chubby policeman. "Kitchen window was open, someone could have gotten in."

The thin policeman said, "We got in ourselves and took a quick look around. There's no one in there, nothing disturbed, no sign of anything being taken."

"I thought it might be those antiques robbers on the TV."

The chubby policeman looked at his friend. "See, I told you—*Crime Call* again! Don't worry, it was probably just the wind—the force must have opened the window, and it's banging now. We'll call the real estate agent tomorrow, get them to fix it." He gave David a stern look. "Don't be so quick to the telephone next time, or you'll find yourself in trouble for wasting police time."

As they headed back toward their car the tall policeman said, "On your own, are you? Where are your parents?"

"My gram had an accident, they had to go away."

"Well, you've got your furry friend there. What's his name?"

"Goliath."

"You shouldn't have any trouble with him looking after you." Because of his sheer size people often assumed Goliath was a trained guard dog. There was no point in explaining that Goliath was

actually rather timid—and pretty stupid sometimes as well.

"Tell you what," said the tall policeman. "We'll be on patrol around here all night. I'll make sure we drive by from time to time. Any problems just get Goliath to bark for help!"

"Thanks, I'll remember that," said David.

The policemen drove away, and David and Goliath went back into the house.

Chapter Three

On the Trail

In the kitchen David gave Goliath a handful of cookies, and made himself some hot chocolate. He was still feeling annoyed by the patronizing attitude of the chubby policeman.

"That fat one said I was wasting his time," he told Goliath indignantly. "They were only in there a few minutes, just flashed their flashlights around and came out. I bet there were lots of perfectly good clues in there and they missed them all." David brooded a while longer, and then came to a decision. "Tell you what, Goliath, we'll go and look for clues ourselves." Goliath looked worried. "It's all right," said David. "The burglars will have been scared off. They must be miles away by now. If we find some clues that lead to the antiques gang getting caught, we might even end up on *Crime Call!*"

Downing his chocolate, David jumped to his feet, went up to his bedroom and got his big flashlight from his closet. He went downstairs and put on his raincoat. "Come on, Goliath!" He opend the front door. It was the proverbial dark and stormy night by now. The wind was whipping the tree tops and David could see the driving rain in the circle of light from the streetlight outside the house.

Goliath gave him a worried look, as if

to say, *"Surely you don't really want me to go out in that?"*

But David did. Grabbing Goliath's collar, he dragged him out into the wind and rain. They hurried next door, went up the wet and muddy path, and followed it around to the back of Mr. MacGregor's house. The police had pulled the window closed, but it was easy to open. David climbed through into the kitchen, and Goliath scrambled after him. Switching on his flashlight, David shone it around the darkened kitchen. He flicked a lightswitch but of course nothing happened. The electricity had been shut off. Goliath whined, as if to say, "This way" and led David into the living room. Standing in the darkness, aware of the shapes of heavy old-fashioned furniture all around him, David suddenly started feeling very scared. Maybe this wasn't such a good idea after all. Suppose there was a lurking burglar, waiting to leap out? David told himself he was being silly. The burglars would have taken off by now, frightened by the police car. He'd just take a very quick look around, and then hurry back home where it was nice and warm and light . . . .

Suddenly David noticed something strange. A beam of light was coming into the room from the streetlight outside. One of the closed velvet curtains had been pulled back, just a little. David shone his flashlight over to the far side of the room. There was a round polished table by the window, with a little chair beside it at an angle. David went over to the table and shone his flashlight on it. The polished surface of the little table was covered with dust and there were marks on it.

One big round one, one smaller round one, and a splash of liquid. David dipped his finger in the liquid and tasted it cautiously. It was tea . . . .

He heard a rustling from underneath the table. Shining his flashlight he saw that Goliath was sniffing at something white. "What have you got there, boy? Give it here!"

Goliath had found a tiny crumpled ball of white paper, marked with greasy stains. "Sandwich paper!" thought David. He examined the little chair and found a sprinkling of crumbs. "Someone's been sitting at this table having tea and sandwiches. Those marks were made by the thermos and the cup!" He peered through the little gap at the edge of the curtain, and found himself looking at the big house across the street.

Puzzled, David shone his flashlight around the room. Nothing else seemed to be out of place—until he shone his flashlight on the big yellow sofa. There was a huge depression on the velvet cushions, as though someone very big and heavy had stretched out on it. David examined the sofa more closely. At one end the sofa cushions were stained with grease. At the other there were the marks of muddy feet. It seemed an awfully long way between the two sets of marks . . . .

"Pay attention, Goliath," said David. "You're Doctor Watson, right? I'm Sherlock Holmes, about to amaze you with my brilliant deductions. Someone very big had a nap on this sofa—while someone else sat in the window watching the house across the street." Goliath whined uneasily.

"How do I know it was two somebodies?" David went on. "Well, anyone big enough to make these marks on the sofa wouldn't have chosen that spindly chair in the window. No, it was two people all right, one very big, the other probably quite small . . . ."

Goliath whined again. Being in the dark in a strange house was making him feel nervous too.

"Quite right, Watson," said David. "We must get back home and tell the police about our amazing discoveries. They'll probably just laugh, but at least we've tried . . . ."

They made their way out of the darkened house and into the wet and windy night. It was raining really hard now, and they were both soaked by the time they reached their own front door. Fishing out his key, David opened the door and they went inside. Goliath shook himself in the hallway, just as he did after a swim, scattering raindrops everywhere. Suddenly he whined, looked anxiously at David, and barked.

"What's the matter?" asked David, hanging up his raincoat. "We're safely home now."

Suddenly he heard voices, people talking, a burst of laughter. "Must have

left the TV on," he thought. "Funny, I could have sworn I turned it off."

He turned and went into the living room, Goliath padding beside him. The television was on—and a little man was watching it. The man wore black pants, a black sweater, and a black jacket. He had a cheerful, rather impish face with a pug nose. He was drinking tea from the cup of a thermos, and munching the remains of a sandwich. Instinctively David spun around and ran for the door—only to bounce off a second man dressed exactly like the first. But this man was so huge he filled the entire doorway. The huge man grabbed David by the shoulders, and shoved him back into the room.

Goliath barked excitedly. *This must be some kind of game. Maybe somebody would get under a rug soon and they could play bears . . . .*

"I do hope that dog's not dangerous," said the little man on the sofa quietly. Suddenly there was a black automatic in the little man's hand. "This is a Walther PPK, just like James Bond's," he said. "Stop an elephant, let alone an overgrown shag rug like that." He leveled the gun at Goliath . . . .

Chapter Four

The Mysterious Intruders

Immediately David went cold. He just
had to convince these intruders Goliath
was harmless. It was true enough after
all. He managed a laugh. "Goliath
dangerous? Don't you believe it. He's
just big that's all. A pat on the back and
a cookie and he's everyone's friend. Sit,
boy! Lie down! Roll over!" Obediently,
Goliath rolled over on his back, and
David tickled his tummy.

"See? He's just a great big softy."

Goliath got up and the big man leaned over and patted him.

"He's cute, ain't he? Can I give him a cookie?" He had a little round head with long greasy hair, a punched-in nose, and a husky, rather child-like voice.

"All right, Jumbo," said the little man impatiently. "Shut up and start watching." Obediently, the big man moved over to the window, pulled back the curtains a few inches and peered out. The smaller man said, "I figure your mom and dad are away, sonny?"

David stared at him, "How did you know that?"

"Heard you tell the cops, didn't I?"

David remembered the lurking figure he'd thought he'd seen.

"You were hiding in the bushes!"

"That's right. Now, when are they coming back?"

"Tomorrow afternoon."

"They just left you alone?"

"A neighbor was coming, but her kid got sick."

The little man thought for a moment. "Are they gonna call you?"

David shrugged. "I don't know—I guess so."

"When they do, you tell them everything's all right. By the time they get back we'll be gone, and no one will get hurt, okay?" David nodded and the little man gave him a hard stare. Then he nodded, apparently satisfied, and put his gun away.

David was feeling pretty scared by now, but he was determined not to show it. And at least Goliath was out of danger.

"You tried to get into the big house across the street, didn't you?" he said.

"Set off the alarms so the police came around. Then you hid out next door and watched the place—till you saw the police car coming back and took off."

"That's right," said the little man cheerfully. "Hid out in the bushes, got soaked. Then we grabbed our tea and sandwiches and slipped in here around the back way while you were messing around next door." He looked around the room. "This is a lot better than hanging around in an empty old house, isn't it, Jumbo. This is much handier."

Suddenly David was feeling more curious than frightened. "Handy for what? You didn't get in across the street, you didn't take anything next door . . . . Why hang around? There's nothing for a gang of antiques robbers in this house."

"Antiques?" said the little man

indignantly. "Wouldn't touch 'em. Too
easily identified—and you have to sell
'em to some crooked dealer for a
fraction of what they're worth. They're
robbers, those dealers. No, take it from
me, son, there's only one thing worth
stealing."

"What's that?"

"Money!"

"I still don't see—"

"Shut up, will you sonny? Stop asking so many questions."

From his place at the window the big man said, "Car coming, Sparrow, could be them."

Sparrow jumped up. "All right, kid, get over there with Jumbo. Take the dog."

David grabbed Goliath by the collar and obeyed.

"Right," said Sparrow. "This is how it works. You keep the dog quiet, Jumbo keeps you quiet. Don't try anything silly, Jumbo doesn't know his own strength."

A ham-sized hand descended on David's shoulder and he stood very still. Goliath looked up baffled, wagging his tail, still waiting for the game to start.

From his place at the window, David saw a car pull up outside the big house across the street. A plump little man got out, and David recognized his new neighbor. The hat and umbrella were gone though, and he was wearing casual weekend clothes. A nice-looking middle-aged woman got out of the passenger seat. Then David heard his own front door open. He saw Sparrow appear in the street, and run up to the newly arrived couple. Sparrow's voice sounded panicky and much more polished than usual. "Please, could you give me some help? There's been an accident in that house over there, people are hurt . . . ."

David opened his mouth—and Jumbo's hand clamped over it. He heard more voices, the sound of footsteps, then Sparrow's voice in the hall. "No, I don't really know what happened, I was just passing myself and I heard someone calling for help . . . ."

The front door slammed, the living room door opened and Sparrow showed the couple into the room. They stopped in amazement at the sight of Jumbo, David, and Goliath.

The man turned. "Say, what's going—"

He broke off at the sight of the gun in Sparrow's hand.

"Sit down and shut up!" said Sparrow quietly.

The man didn't seem to believe his eyes. "Now look here—"

"Jumbo!" snapped Sparrow.

Releasing David, Jumbo grabbed the two newcomers, one in each hand, and threw them onto the sofa.

Sparrow looked at David. "Now do you understand?"

"Not really."

"Don't you know who this is?"

"It's the man from across the street."

Sparrow sighed. "That's the trouble these days, people don't talk to their neighbors any more. No sense of community. This, sonny, is Mr. Morris, manager of your friendly main street bank!"

Suddenly David understood. "I see! You were on *Crime Call*, but I got the wrong ones. You're not antiques thieves, you're the bank robbers!"

Sparrow stood menacingly over Mr. Morris, who still seemed quite stunned. "All right then, this is how it works. Tonight we all stay here. First thing tomorrow, you and I go to the bank, you open the safe and give me the cash."

"There's a time lock," said Mr. Morris desperately.

"Switches itself off at half past eight. We reach the bank at quarter after, I'm gone with the loot by eight forty-five." He jabbed the gun at Mr. Morris. "You stay at the bank, act as though nothing's happened. I come back here, pick up Jumbo and we're gone. Your wife gives you a call and it's all over. No one gets hurt—if you're all sensible. And remember this," He looked at David and Goliath, then at Mr. and Mrs. Morris. "Each of you two is responsible for the other. One of you tries anything, the other one pays, understand?"

David looked around the little group of his fellow prisoners. He understood all right. They were all hostages.

Chapter Five

Goliath's Big Moment

No one said anything. "All right," said
Sparrow. "How about a nice cup of tea?
Jumbo, take the kid in the kitchen and—"

The telephone rang—and rang.

"That'll be my parents," said David.
"If nobody answers . . . ."

Sparrow nodded. "All right. But be
careful."

David picked up the phone. "Mom?
Yes, I'm fine. How's Gram?"

His mother's voice seemed to come

from a different world. Gram was much better and would be out of the hospital soon.

"Where's Sue?" said his mother. "Can I speak to her?"

"Billy got a bit over-excited and Sue's trying to get him to sleep, so I'd rather not call her. No, everything's fine, I'm just going to bed . . . ."

Mr. Morris was middle-aged, plump with glasses, but no one could say he lacked spirit. Suddenly he leaped to his feet and made a grab for the phone. He was opening his mouth to shout when Jumbo's fist hit him under the chin, and he crashed to the ground. Goliath started barking excitedly.

Sparrow's gun was pointing not at David but at Goliath.

"Hang on a sec, Mom," shouted David. "Down, Goliath, sit! Quiet, boy!"

Goliath subsided, whining uneasily. David returned to the phone. "Sorry about all that, just old Goliath being crazy as usual. He got excited playing with Billy and he's missing him. He came dashing into the room and knocked over a chair. No, he's okay. Speak, Goliath!" Now thoroughly confused, Goliath delivered a few barks into the phone. "All right, that'll do," said David. "Goodbye, Mom, see you tomorrow. No, I won't be late for school . . . ."

David put down the phone and looked at Sparrow. "Best I could do. I think they bought it."

Sparrow hesitated, then nodded. "Okay. It'd better work."

Mrs. Morris was fussing over her husband, who was already recovering and sitting up. Suddenly they heard the sound of a car in the street.

Jumbo leaped to the curtains. "It's the cops, Sparrow! They're slowing down . . . ."

"Don't panic, they're only patrolling," whispered David. "They said they'd drive by."

Sparrow waved his gun in an arc. "Dead quiet and dead still all of you, till they move on."

David moved over to Goliath. "I'll just make sure he stays quiet." He put an arm around Goliath's neck. "Now whatever you do," he whispered, "you mustn't . . . speak, Goliath."

Goliath cocked his head at the last two words.

"That's right," whispered David.

Suddenly he shouted, *"Speak, Goliath! Speak!"*

The excited Goliath delivered a whole series of his specials, deep crashing barks that shook the whole house.

Sparrow swung around aiming his gun, and David sprang forward, pushing his arm up. The gun exploded with an enormous bang and plaster showered down from the ceiling.

Mrs. Morris gave a scream that rattled the window panes. Jumbo rushed towards her with a roar—and Mr. Morris executed a low football tackle that brought Jumbo crashing down like a tree. David was still clinging desperately to Sparrow's gun arm. The little man gave him a savage smack on the ear with his other hand. David gave a yell of pain—and something happened to Goliath. Dogs are very sensitive to atmosphere, and Goliath had been feeling unhappy for some time. Somehow he knew David didn't really like these new visitors, and they didn't seem to want to play after all.

When he saw David get hit and heard
him yell, long-buried instincts surfaced
in Goliath. He sprang at Sparrow,
knocking him to the ground, and

sending the gun flying from his hand. As Sparrow struggled to get up, Goliath planted both paws on his chest and gave a low blood-curdling growl. Goliath's fur was standing on end, his eyes glowed red, and he gave another terrifying snarl.

"You said he wasn't dangerous," gasped Sparrow.

"I lied," said David calmly. "He's actually a trained Albanian Mountain Guard Dog, he's half wolf and he's hungry. One move and he'll eat you!"

Sparrow froze and, rubbing his sore ear, David looked around.

Watched approvingly by Mrs. Morris, Mr. Morris was sitting on Jumbo's chest, holding his ears and happily banging his head on the floor. Shouts and loud knocking could be heard from the front door.

"I think your husband's feeling better, Mrs. Morris," said David politely. "Would you like to let the police in?"

The police came crashing in, there were all kinds of explanations, and Sparrow and Jumbo were carted off in the police car. David phoned his parents who insisted on coming home at once. Mr. and Mrs. Morris insisted on staying with David until they arrived, so David got them a cup of tea. It seemed the least he could do.

When they were drinking it, Mrs. Morris noticed that Goliath had disappeared. "What's happened to that wonderful dog of yours?"

"He'll be patrolling the rest of the house," said David solemnly. "Trained guard dog, you know, he never rests. I'll just check up on him. Help yourselves to more tea . . . ."

It had all been too much for poor old Goliath—his nerves had been thoroughly jangled. Dragged out in the rain, sinister visitors, loud bangs and shouts, noisy policemen, told to shut up, told to bark . . . . He took refuge in his usual hiding place at times of stress and it was there David found him.

Lying flat on the floor David grabbed Goliath by the collar, and heaved him out from under the bed. "They're going to make a big deal about you tomorrow, Goliath, and this time you really deserve it. Just for once, you were a genuine hero!"

David gave Goliath a big hug. Goliath, embarrassed by all the praise, gave him a big sloppy kiss . . . .

About the Author

After studying at Cambridge, Terrance
Dicks became an advertising copywriter,
then a radio and television scriptwriter
and script editor. His career as an author
began with the *Dr. Who* series and he has
now written a variety of other books on
subjects ranging from horror to detection.
Barron's publishes several of his series,
including *The Adventures of Goliath*, *T.R.
Bear*, *A Cat Called Max*, and *The MacMagics*.